KB176314

엘리트 시선 45

# 담배꽃 이야기

장현경 시집

엘리트출판사

# 담배꽃 이야기

장 현 경 시집

엘리트출판사

# 아름다운 꽃들의 이야기 3

9월을 보내고 10월을 맞으며, 천고마비의 계절, 가을을 그려 본다. 글을 잘 쓰는 방법에는 여러 가지가 있다고 하겠다. 글쓰기에서는 자신의 노력과 관심이 중요하다. 그리고 글쓰기에 대한 두려움을 없애야 한다. 즉 많이 읽고 쓰고 생각해야 좋은 글을 쓸 수 있다. 그리하여 글쓰기가 만만하게 보여야 한다. 다작(多作), 다독(多讀), 다사(多思)를 되풀이하면 글쓰기가 쉬워 보인다. 반복할수록 '글쓰기가 이렇게 쉬웠던가?'를 느끼게 된다. 가을은 독서하기가 쉬운 계절이다.

1948년 노벨문학상을 탄 시인 T. S. 엘리엇은 "황무지(荒蕪地)"에서 '4월은 잔인한 달'이라고 노래했다. 즉 1차 세계대전으로 인한 폐허의 땅에서 이를 극복해가는 인간의 삶이, 겨울의 혹독한 추위를 이겨내며 새싹을 피워내는 초목처럼 강인하다는 의미일 것이다. 다시 말해 4계절 피는 '아름다운 꽃들의 이야기'가 인간 삶의 어려움을 이겨내는 반려자가 되고자 한다.

　꽃을 보니 눈이 시원해지고 마음도 밝아지고 기분마저 좋아진
다. 시인으로 움츠린 몸에 기지개를 켜며 사계절 지지 않는 꽃들
의 이야기를 소재로 여기 한 권의 영역 시집을 다듬는다. 꽃들의
이야기가 이 어려운 시대를 견뎌내는 수많은 독자에게 위로와
희망, 감동이 되기를 기대합니다.

　늘 따뜻한 성원을 보내주신 가족과 이웃의 지지에 고마운 마음
전하며 청계문학 가족 여러분의 건승을 빕니다. 나의 시편들을
만나는 존경하는 독자님께 건강과 행복이 늘 함께하시기를 기원
합니다.

<br>

2021년 9월 청계서재(淸溪書齋)에서
자정(紫井) 장현경(張鉉景) 삼가 씀

# The Story of Beautiful Flowers 3

We spend September and welcome October, and imagine autumn in the season of the sky is high and the horse is fat. There are many ways to write well. In writing, one's own effort and interest are important. And get rid of the fear of writing. In other words, you need to read, write, and think a lot to write a good article. So, the writing should look good. It seems that writing is easy if you repeat prolific writing, multiple reading, and multiple thinking. The more you repeat it, the more you feel, 'Was writing this easy?' Autumn is an easy season to read.

The poet T. S. Eliot, who won the Novel Prize for Literature in 1948 sang in "The Waste Land" 'April is a cruel month.' In other words, It would mean that human life overcoming this in the ruins of the First World War is as strong as a plant sprouting sprouts overcoming the harsh cold of winter. In other words, 'The Story of Beautiful Flowers', Which blooms in four seasons, aims to become a companion who overcomes the difficulties of human life.

Seeing flowers refreshes my eyes, brightens my heart, and improves my mood. I stretch my body as a poet and refine a book of poems translated into English here with the story of flowers that do not fade in the four seasons. It is hoped that the story of flowers will provide comfort, hope, and inspiration to many readers who are enduring these difficult times.

I would like to express my gratitude to the support of my family and neighbors who have always given me warm support, and I wish the Cheonggye Literature family all the best. To my dear readers who meet my psalms, I wish you good health and good fortune.

September 2021 in Cheonggye Library
Jajeong, **Jang Hyun-kyung** Raising

# 수레국화

어느 왕비가
외세의 침략을 받자

파란색
분홍색
흰색
자주색 수레국화꽃이 핀 들판에
자신의 자녀를 숨겼다

그리고
화살 깃을 동그랗게
꽂아놓은 듯한
수레바퀴 모양의 왕관을 씌워줬다

황제의 꽃이 된
수레국화가
마치 보호가 되는 듯

들판에 널려진 수레국화는
아름다운 한 폭의 그림

자연스럽게
독일과 에스토니아의
국화(國花)가 되었네!

# Cornflower

Which queen
To be invaded by foreign powers

Blue
Pink
White
In the field with purple cornflowers
Hid her own children

And
Round arrow feathers
As if plugged in
She gave me a crown in the shape of a wagon wheel

The Emperor's flower
Cornflower
As if protected

Cornflowers in the field
A beautiful picture

Naturally
Germany and Estonia
It has become the national flower!

## contents

# 제1부  라능쿨러스꽃

# 제2부 글라디올러스꽃

# 제3부 부처꽃

# 제4부 담배꽃 이야기

# 제5부 배롱나무꽃

# 제1부

# 라눙쿨러스꽃

매혹적이다 / 크림색 도는 꽃
꽃잎이 300장

# 야래향꽃

밤에 꽃이 피고
향기를 터트리는
예쁜 꽃 무리

해님 보고
내외하던 풀꽃 아가씨

짙은 향기로
정인을 유혹하여
겸연쩍게 미소 짓는
달빛 그림자

아침이면
오므라들어
밤낮이 바뀐
말 없는 사랑.

# Yarae Incense Flower

Flower bloom at night
Smelling
Pretty bunch of flowers

Watching the sun
The flower girl who was out and about

With a strong scent
By seducing
Humbly smiling
Moonlight shadow

In the morning
Shrink
Night and day changed
Love without words.

# 하늘타리꽃

저녁 어스름에
순백으로 활짝 피어
그 앙증스러움에 행복을 느낀다

다음날 오후가 되면
지는 꽃으로

덩굴손이 있어
하늘 높이 올라간다

담장이나 울타리에서
싱그럽고 소박하게 피어
자리를 지킨 하늘타리꽃

비 오는 날엔
우수에 젖어
더 귀엽구나!

# Sky Flower

In the evening twilight
Blooming in pure white
I feel happy with that ugliness

The next afternoon
With a falling flower

Have tendrils
Rise high in the sky

On a fence or fence
Fresh and simple bloom
The sky lily flower that kept its place

On a rainy day
Soaked in rain
You're cuter!

# 목단꽃

흰색 붉은색이 노란색과 어울려
부와 명예의 상징으로
꽃 중의 꽃
오늘을 맞는다

화려하고 풍요로워
은은하게 향기가 흐르는 꽃 중의 왕
5월에 현란하게 피어
예술가들의 가슴을
설레게 한다

부귀영화를 누렸다는 듯이
세월이 흘러
목단 꽃잎이 하나둘
떨어진다.

# Magnolia Flower

White red goes well with yellow
As a symbol of wealth and honor
Flower among flower
Meet today

Colorful and rich
The king of flowers with a soft fragrance
Blooms brilliantly in May
The hearts of artists
Excite

As if enjoying wealth and wealth
Years pass
One by one wood petals
Falls.

# 라눙쿨러스꽃

미나리 같은 줄기에
장미를 닮은 라눙쿨러스
봄을 아는 듯
예쁘게 꽃이 핀다

매혹적이다
크림색 도는 꽃
꽃잎이 300장

색상마다
무척 화려한 인상을 주어
애지중지 보고 싶었던 꽃

와!
그대는 꽃 중의 여왕!

# Ranunculus Flower

On a stalk like a water parsley
Ranunclus resembling a rose
Seems to know spring
Bloom beautifully

Enchanting
Cream-colored flower
300 petals

Per color
Give a very splendid impression
The flower that I wanted to cherish and see

And!
You are the queen of flowers!

# 꽃다지꽃

이른 봄에 피는 꽃
꽃대가 늘어나며
꽃망울이 올망졸망

봄바람에 넘실대는
노란색 물결

카메라 화면이
노랗게 물들고

눈동자에도
노란색 세상이 펼쳐진다

포근한 땅에
예쁜 꽃으로 피어나

주변의 무관심에도
꽃다지꽃 무리는
찬란한 불꽃놀이.

# Lotus Flower

Flowers blooming in early spring
Flower stalks increase
The flower buds are all over the place

Fluttering in the spring wind
Yellow wave

The camera screen
Dyed yellow

Even in the eyes
A yellow world unfolds

On the warm ground
Blooming with pretty flowers

In spite of the indifference around
Bunch of flowers
Brilliant fireworks.

# 냉이꽃

저 산 그늘에
하얗게 눈이 쌓여 있고
찬 바람이 부는 이른 봄날에

길가나 밭둑에서
흔히 보이는 나생이

쑥과 경쟁하듯이
키 재기를 하고

새색시 보조개 닮은 냉이꽃처럼
하얗게 미소지으며
맛 나는 반찬으로
봄 향기를 흩날린다

냉이 김치
냉이된장국

이른 봄에
잊을 수 없는
맛 나는 냉이 나물!

# Cold Flower

In the shade of that mountain
Snow is piled up white
On a cold windy early spring day

On the roadside or in the field
Commonly seen Nasaeng

As if competing with mugwort
Do a key

Like a wassy flower resembling a dimple
Smiling white
As a delicious side dish
The scent of spring scatters

Wasabi kimchi
Cold miso soup

In early spring
Unforgettable
Delicious wasabi herbs!

# 달래꽃

봄이 지나고
초여름에
들판에서 만난 달래꽃

힘차게 뻗은
긴 꽃대가 산들바람에
흔들흔들

연분홍으로 동그랗게
핀 꽃 한 송이

자세히 보니
파꽃보다 훨씬
야리야리하고 신비롭다

마치 별꽃들이 모여
빛이 반짝반짝
정말로 예쁘다

독특한 맛과 향취를
지닌 채!

# Wild Rocambole Flower

Spring is over
In early summer
A flower found in the field

Outstretched
Long flower stalks in the breeze
Shake

Round in pink
A blooming flower

I looked closely
Much more than green
Sassy and mysterious

Like star flowers
Light is twinkling
Really pretty

Unique taste and smell
With it!

# 쑥부쟁이꽃

그리움이 사무치는
하얀 쑥부쟁이꽃

산과 들에 군락을 지어
수줍게 피어있네

바람결에 춤을 추듯
곱게 핀 쑥부쟁이꽃
흰색과 보랏빛으로
지천에 널려 있고

저무는 들녘에는
더욱더 향기 은은하네

집 담장 아래
울타리 옆에
소박하고 청초하게
피어 있는 쑥부쟁이꽃

이 땅의 가을을
더욱 가을 하게 하네!

# Mugwort Flower

Longing for
White mugwort flower

Build a colony in the mountains and field
Shyly blooming

Like dancing in the wind
A finely bloomed mugwort flower
In white and purple
Are scattered all over the

In the setting field
The scent is more subtle

Under the house wall
Next to the fence
Simple and neat
Blooming mugwort flower

Autumn in this land
It makes it even more autumn!

# 왕고들빼기꽃

한해살이풀들과 섞여
키가 커
돋보일 무렵

인적이 드문
아무데서나 잘 자라는
참 예쁜
왕고들빼기꽃

한여름 무더위에
쌉쌀하고 부드러운 잎으로
삼겹살 쌈
뿌리로
달짝지근한 반찬
오로지
인간을 향한 그리움으로

환하게 미소를 짓는
모정(慕情)의 꽃.

# Lactuca Indica Flower

Mixed with annuals
Tall
When you stand out

Sparsely populated
Growing anywhere
Very pretty
Lactuca Indica Flower

In the midsummer heat
With bitter and soft leaves
Samgyeopsal Wrap
By root
Sweet side dish
Only
With longing for humanity

Smiling brightly
A mother's flower.

담배꽃 이야기

# 제2부

# 글라디올러스꽃

층층이 같은 색으로 / 경쟁하듯
빨강, 분홍, 연초록, 노랑, 보라색으로 / 피워 올려

# 복수초꽃

겨우내 다진 그리움으로
솟아오른 진한 생명의 혼
봄눈으로 품어 녹이고

그 위를
이른 봄바람이 스친다

엄동설한 숨죽였던 생명
하얀 그리움에 수줍은 듯
시린 가슴 달래며
얼굴 내민 샛노란 복수초

찬바람이 떠나기 전
뭇 봄꽃들의 개화를 이끌려
노란 눈꽃으로
이정표를 세우네!

# Amur Adonis Flower

With the longing that has been crushed in the past
Soaring deep soul of life
Embrace it with spring snow and melt it

Above it
The early spring wind blows

A life that held its breath
Seems shy with white longing
Soothing my aching chest
A bright yellow plentiful plant with a face out

Before the cold wind leaves
Leading the blooming of all spring flowers
With yellow snowflakes
Set milestones!

# 글라디올러스꽃

글라디올러스
키가 1m

여러해살이풀 중에
모범이 되려는 듯

하늘을 향해
한줄기로 솟아오르며
꽃을 피운다

층층이 같은 색으로
경쟁하듯
빨강, 분홍, 연초록, 노랑, 보라색으로
피워 올려

온 천지에
글라디올러스꽃

돋보이네!

# Gladiolus Flower

Gladiolus
1m tall

Among the perennials
Like to be an example

Towards the sky
Rising in a single line
Bloom

Layer by layer in the same color
As if competing
Red, pink, light green, yellow, purple
Light it up

All over the sky
Gladiolus flower

It stands out!

# 개망초꽃

저 멀리
북아메리카에서 시집온
귀화 식물

이 땅에 뿌리내리려
비바람에
온갖 고초를 겪은 꽃

보이지 않는 시달림에도
고난의 눈물을 견디고
우아하게 자라난 꽃

세월이 흘러
아무 데서나 무더기로 자라나
소소(疎疎)하고 청초한 모습

경건한 마음으로
사랑스러운 눈빛으로
너를 바라본다.

# Sagebrush Flower

Far away
Married in North America
Naturalized plant

To take root in this land
In the rain
A flower that has gone through all kinds of hardships

Even in invisible suffering
Endure the tears of suffering
A flower that grows gracefully

Years pass
Growing in heaps everywhere
Insignificant and neat look

With a reverent heart
with lovely eyes
Looking at you.

# 홀아비바람꽃

저승으로 간 아내가
남긴 흔적

가슴을 촉촉이 적시는
바람꽃

남편을 위해
하얗게
아름다운 자태로

숲속의 봄을
홀아비바람꽃으로
장식하여
애잔함을 달랜다.

# Widower Wind Flower

Wife who went to the underworld
Traces left behind

Moisten the chest
Wind flower

For her husband
White
In a beautiful way

Spring in the forest
With a widower's flower
To decorate
Salvage the cuteness.

# 이팝나무꽃

이팝나무가

올 한 해
풍년 농사를 위해

초여름에
가로수 좌우로

하얗게 꽃을
수놓고 싶어 하네!

# Poplar Flower

This poplar tree

This year
For a  bountiful harvest

In early summer
Roadside tree from side to side

White flowers
It wants to embroider!

# 파고다꽃

히말라야 산간 지역에
400년마다
한 번씩 피는 파고다꽃

힘이 있고
신령스러워

살아생전에 볼 수 있다면
행운일 수도 있지만

우리 주변
아름다운 꽃 중에도
행운의 꽃이
많이 있지 않을까?

# Pagoda Flower

In the Himalayas
Every 400 years
Pagoda flowers that blooms once

There is power
It's divine

If I could see you before I was alive
May be lucky

Around us
Among the beautiful flowers
Lucky flower
Will there be many?

# 괴마옥(怪魔玉)꽃

봄에 피는 괴마옥꽃
앙증맞게 귀엽다

언뜻 보니
파인애플처럼 생겨
꽃이 아닌 듯

거친 몸집에
여기저기
싹이 돋아
꽃봉오리와 잎이 비슷하네

노랗게 핀 괴마옥꽃
귀신을 쫓는 꽃
이름과 달리
볼수록 예뻐
더욱 신기하네!

# Monster Jade Flower

Monstrous jade flower blooming in spring
Adorable

I looked frozen
Looks like a pineapple
Doesn't look like a flower

In a rough body
Here and there
Sprout
Like flower buds and leaves

Yellow magnolia flower
Flower chasing ghosts
Contrary to the name
The more I look, the more beautiful
It's even more exciting!

# 히아신스꽃

꽃은 사랑이다

히아신스는 영원한 사랑이다
보살펴야 하는 어린이다

초록에서 보랏빛으로
꽃 빛이 변할 때
천연 방향제 같은 향기를 흩날리며

봄이 오면
사랑의 생명을 소생시키듯
예쁘게 핀다

생화보다는 매력이 있어
밤 분위기에 잘 어울리는
감미로운 히아신스꽃!

# Hyacinth Flower

Flowers are love

Hyacinth is eternal love
A child to be looked after

From green to purple
When the flower light changes
Scattering the fragrance like a natural air freshener

When spring comes
As if reviving the life of love
Bloom beautifully

There's more to it than a live flower
Perfect for the night atmosphere
Sweet hyacinth flowers!

# 야생화

산과 들
길 위
어디에서나 피는 들꽃

어디서 왔는지
돌보지 않아도
잘 자란다

우리가 보는
정원의 아름다운 꽃들도
태생적으로 야생화에서
비롯된 꽃들

야생화를 닮아
힘차게
영역을 넓혀 가고 있는.

# Wild Flower

Mountains and fields
On the road
Wild flowers blooming everywhere

Where did you come from
Without caring
Grow well

We see
Beautiful flowers in the garden
Natively in the wild
Flowers from

Resembling wild flowers
Lively
Expanding the realm.

# 달리아꽃

갖가지 색깔의 꽃

흰색과 주홍
연핑크
빨강
붉은빛 보라

무더운 날씨에도
둥글고 예쁘게 피는 꽃

줄지어 피는 달리아에
설레는 마음과 향기로 인해
젊어지는 느낌이 가득

달리아 심으러
꽃밭에 가야지

내 마음속에
가지고 싶은 달리아!

# Dahlia Flower

Different colored flower

White and scarlet
Light pink
Red
Red purple

Even in hot weather
Round and beautiful flowers

Rows of blooming dahlias
Because of the fluttering heart and scent
Full of rejuvenation

To plant dahlias
I'm going to the flower garden

In my mind
I want to have dahlias!

# 마타리꽃

가끔 만나는
여러해살이풀
여름꽃 마타리

여름에서 가을까지
노란색 마타리 우산 꽃
산방꽃차례(繖房꽃次例)를 이룬다

꽃대가 길어 말 다리
말 타리
마타리가 된 순 우리 말

어린 순은 나물
전초는 약재로 쓰이며

어디서나
무리를 지어
바람이 불면
노랑 물결을 이룬다.

# Matari Flower

Meet occasionally
Perennial herb
Summer flower matari

From summer to autumn
Yellow matari umbrella flower
Forms an inflorescence

Horse legs with long flower stalks
Horse ride
The pure Korean words that became Matari

Young sterling greens
The herb is used medicinally

Anywhere
Flock
When the wind blows
Yellow ripples.

담배꽃 이야기

# 제3부

## 부처꽃

자세히 보면 / 결실을 보지 못하고
이별한 슬픈 사랑 이야기

# 백일홍 붉은 꽃

가을이 왔다
눈을 떠보니 가을이다
단풍 길이 생각난다

창문을 열고
알몸으로 기지개 켜면

올 것만 같아
누군가
올 듯만 싶어

바라만 보아도 가슴에 번져오는
백일홍 붉은 물결
벌겋게 타오르는 정염(情炎)

만나고 싶은 이
누군가 올 듯도 한
그런 날이 기다려지네!

# Crimson Red Flower

Autumn has come
When I open my eyes, it's autumn
Reminds me of autumn leaves

Open the window
When you stretch out naked

It seems to come
Someone
I just want to come

Just looking at it, it spreads in my heart
Crimson red wave
Burning passion

I want to meet
As if someone would come
I look forward to that day.

# 사프란꽃

사프란 묘목
한 번 심어 놓으면
그늘이나 메마른 땅에서도
잘 자라

공기 나쁜 도심에서도
찌푸리지 않고
물 주지 않아도
절대로 탓하지 않는다

차라리 시들어 죽을지라도

처음 꽃이 필 때
황금색 암술머리를 안고
여러 색상으로 피는 꽃

사프란 차로 죽음에서 벗어나는
청초한 번홍화(蕃紅花)

비늘줄기를 꺾어도
진한 향기를 잃지 않는다.

# Saffron Flower

Saffron seedlings
Once planted
Even in the shade or in dry land
Good night

Even in the city with bad air
Without frown
Even without water
Never blame

I'd rather wither and die

When the first flowers bloom
Holding golden stigma
Flowers blooming in multiple colors

Escaping death with saffron tea
Neat and clean safflower.

Even if you break the scales
It does not lose its strong scent.

# 달개비꽃

가을!

달개비가 가을을
빛깔로 알리고 있다

암수 한 몸에
가냘픈 꽃송이

가까이 다가가
휴대폰 카메라로
한 컷 찰칵!

# Moonflower

Autumn!

Moongae in autumn
Announce with color

Male and female body
Slender flower

Get close
With cell phone camera
One click

# 옥잠화

휘영청 달밤에
널려 있는 옥잠화

초록색으로 덮인 잎 위에
드문드문
꽃대 하나로
피어오른 하얀 꽃

가지고 싶은
옥비녀 꽃봉오리

입술 여는 어스름 저녁에
활짝 핀 옥잠화

밤을 새우다 지쳐
아침이면 시든 옥잠화

외로운 나날을 보내는
순결한 여인의 영혼이여!

# Daylily

Hwiyoungcheong on the moonlit night
Scattered daylilies

On the green-covered leaves
Sparsely
One flower stalk
Blooming white flowers

Want to have
Jade hairpin flower bud

On a twilight evening when you open your lips
Daylily in full bloom

Tired of staying up all night
Daylilies that wither in the morning

Spending lonely days
Soul of a pure woman!

# 설유화

꽃샘추위에
봄을 알리는 하얀 꽃
춘설로 피고 지고

가까이서 보면
눈꽃이 핀 듯

멀리서 보면
날아갈 듯
하얀 날개

먼저 피는 꽃
나중에 돋는 이파리

바람에도 꿋꿋이
나비가 춤을 추는 듯
눈이 부시는 야생화.

# Snow Oil Painting

In the cold spring
White flowers heralding spring
Blooming and losing due to the spring snow

Look closely
Like a snowflake

From a distance
like to fly
White wings

Flower that blooms first
Leaves that sprout later

Steadfast in the wind
Like a butterfly dancing
Dazzling wildflowers.

# 엉겅퀴꽃

온몸에 촘촘히
가시가 많아
가시 같지 않지만
날카로워 보인다

두상꽃차례로
무리 지어 피우려
산야에 홀로 서서
비바람을 맞는다

오래도록 함께하자고
보랏빛으로
몸을 흔들며
오묘한 향기를 흩날린다.

# Thistle Flower

All over the body
A lot of thorns
It's not like a thorn
Looks sharp

In an inflorescence
To smoke in a crowd
Standing alone in the mountains
Rain and wind

Let's be together for a long time
In purple
Waving
Scatters a strange scent.

# 초롱꽃

불혹(不惑)에 이르도록
나는
성실하지 못했다

아니
감사할 줄 모르며 살아왔다

세월이 흘러
얼마나 더 살면

감사와 성실을
가슴에 품은 초롱꽃처럼
될 수 있을까!

# Lantern Flower

To lead to unhappiness
I
I was not sincere

No
I've been living without being grateful

Years pass
How much longer do you live

Thanks and sincerity
Like a lantern flower in my chest
Could it be!

# 부처꽃

작고 예쁜 야생화
한여름 무더위를 이겨내고
산책로 주변 연못가에
저마다의 몸짓으로

앙증스럽게
피어 있는 부처꽃

자세히 보면
결실을 보지 못하고
이별한 슬픈 사랑 이야기

붉은 자줏빛 꽃잎
연꽃과 색상이 비슷하여
연꽃 공양 대신으로
쓰인 부처꽃.

# Buddha Flower

Small and pretty wildflowers
Beat the midsummer heat
By the pond near the promenade
With each gesture

Hatefully
Blooming buddha

Look closely
Not seeing results
Sad love story

Red purple petals
The color is similar to that of a lotus flower
Instead of offering lotus flowers
Used buddha flower.

# 구기자나무꽃

1년에 두 번 꽃이 피는
구기자나무꽃

여름에 한 번 피며
열매 맺고
가을에 한 번 더 꽃이 핀다

뿌리껍질은 해열제로
줄기는 차(茶)로
어린잎은 나물이나 반찬으로
열매는 술을 만들고
말려서 불로장수하는 약재로 쓴다

하나 버릴 것 없는
구기자나무
봉사와 희생정신이 강해

함께 사랑하며
살아가려무나!

# Wolfberry Flower

Blooms twice a year
Wolfberry Flower

Blooms once in summer
Bear fruit
Flowers bloom once more in the fall

The root bark is an antipyretic
The stem is tea
The young leaves can be used as a side dish
The fruits make wine
It is dried and used as a medicine for longevity

Nothing to throw away
Wolfberry tree
Strong spirit of service and sacrifice

Love together
I want to live!

# 팬지꽃차

팬지꽃차를 즐겨 마시면
당신을 버리지 않아요

뇌 질환을 예방하고
피부 노화를 개선하고
암 예방은 물론
활성산소도 제거한다

가끔
눈 건강에도 좋고
관절염이나 방광염
불면증 완화에도 쓰인다

하양 노랑 보라로
생각에 잠긴 얼굴을 하고 있는
팬지꽃

쾌활한 모습으로
우리에게
환한 웃음을 주리리.

# Pansy Flower Tea

If you enjoy drinking pansy flower tea
I won't leave you

Prevent brain disease
Improve skin aging
Cancer prevention, of course
It also removes active oxygen

Sometimes
Good for eye health
Arthritis or cystitis
It is also used to relieve insomnia

White yellow purple
With a thoughtful face
Pansy flower

In a cheerful manner
To us
I will give you a bright smile.

담배꽃 이야기

# 제4부

# 담배꽃 이야기

세월이 흘러도 / 사람들은 예쁜 담배꽃을
본적이 별로 없다.

# 목화꽃

장맛비 갠 하늘에
뭉게구름 둥실둥실
나뭇잎이 무성하게
흩날릴 무렵

저 넓은 들판에
목화꽃 하얗게 피어나

한여름 삼복더위가
끝나갈 건들팔월에

다래가 주렁주렁
영글어 터지면

하얀 꽃송이가
햇빛에 반짝반짝

목화밭에서
목화 따는 아낙네

한 폭의 그림을
떠올리게 하네!

# Cotton Flower

In the rainy sky
Puffy clouds
Leaves lush
When it scatters

On that wide field
Cotton flowers bloom white

The midsummer heat
Things that will end in August

The sand is piled high
If English explodes

White flowers
Shining in the sunlight

In the cotton field
A woman picking cotton

One wide picture
Reminds me!

# 어저귀꽃

세월이 흘러
때가 때이니만큼

예전보다
어촌의 배가
너무나 발전해버린 요즘

밧줄이라고

오래전에
야생화 어저귀꽃의 줄기로
밧줄을 만들어 쓰다니

거짓인 듯
믿을 수 없다는 듯

보아야겠다고
옛날에 썼던 밧줄을!

# Abutilon Flower

Years pass
As the time is the time

Than before
Fishing village boat
These days, we have developed so much

Called a rope

A long time ago
With the stem of a wild abutilon flower
Making a rope

Seems to be a lie
Can't seem to believe it

I want to see
The rope I used in the past!

# 수박풀꽃

나른한 아침 햇살에
길 숲을 헤치니
고요가 흐른다

아름답고 진실한 사랑의 꽃

물안개가
피어오르는 듯한 눈동자
매혹적으로 보이는 듯

줄기는 흰털이 나고
이파리는 수박을 닮아
여기저기 곱게 핀
아이보리 수박풀꽃

내 마음을 유혹하네!

# Watermelon Flower

In the languid morning sun
I walk through the forest
Silence flows

Beautiful and true love flower

Water mist
Blooming eyes
Looks seductive

Stems are white
The leaves resemble watermelon
Finely bloomed everywhere
Ivory watermelon flower

You seduce my heart

# 안스리움꽃

갑자기
안스리움꽃들을 만나면
온몸에 달려드는 맑은 공기로
전율한다

빨간 입술은
불타는 가슴을 보여주는 듯
사랑을 꽃피우고

수술은
용암을 분출하는
살아 있는 생명

빨강 하양 핑크
꽃들을 에워싸는
녹색 이파리들의 몸부림

5월의 장미꽃보다
붉은
불같은 사랑의 고백

목마른 내 마음에
불길처럼 타올라
한줄기의 힘찬 그리움으로!

# Anthurium Flower

Suddenly
When you meet anthurium flowers
With the fresh air rushing all over your body
Tremble

The red lips
As if showing a burning heart
Make love bloom

Stamen is
Erupting lava
Living life

Red white pink
Surrounded by flowers
The writhing of green leaves

Than the rose in May
Red
Confession of fiery love

In my thirsty heart
Burn like fire
With a single strong longing!

# 담배꽃 이야기

참으로 못생긴
인디언 소녀가 있었다

못 난 외모로
한 번도 사랑할 수가 없었네

마음씨는 아름다웠지만
모든 남자는 그녀에게
고개를 돌려
결국 유언을 남기고 자살을 선택한다

"다음 세상엔
모든 남자와 키스하고 싶다"

얼마 후
소녀가 죽은 자리에
담배라는 풀이 돋아났다

소녀의 소원대로
남자들은 담배와 무수히 키스했다

빨갛게 달아오른 담배꽃
담뱃잎의 성장을 방해하므로

꽃이 피기 전에
꽃망울을 잘라낸다

세월이 흘러도
사람들은 예쁜 담배꽃을
본적이 별로 없다.

# Tobacco Flower Story

Really ugly
There was an indian girl

With ugly looks
I've never been able to love

My heart was beautiful
All her men tell her
Turn her head
She eventually leaves her will and chooses to commit suicide

"In the next world
I want to kiss every man"

After a while
Where the girl died
The grass called tobacco has sprouted

According to the girl's wish
Men kissed cigarettes countless times

Red hot tobacco flower
It inhibits the growth of tobacco leaves

Before the flowers bloom
Cut the flower buds

Even if the years pass
People make pretty tobacco flowers
I haven't seen much.

# 옥수수꽃

비가 그치고
햇빛이 쨍쨍

산책길에서 본 옥수수
가까이 다가가

"너는 이름이 뭐니?"
물어본다
대답이 없다

큰 키는 동무하려는 듯
옥수수꽃과 마주 보니

벌 나비 날아들고

머지않아
튼실해진 옥수수
하모니카가 생각난다

그해 여름날
김이 모락모락
쪄낸 옥수수
하모니카 소리가 들리는 듯.

# Corn Flower

The rain stops
The sun is shining

Corn seen on the promenade
Get close

"What is your name?"
I ask
No answer

Big stature seems to want to mate
Facing the corn flower

Bee butterfly flying

Soon
Hardened corn
Reminds me of harmonica

That summer day
Steaming
Steamed corn
It sounds like a harmonica.

# 시스투스꽃

흰색 자주 분홍색으로 피는
여기 아름답고
인기 있는 시스투스꽃

주변에 식물이 번성하거나
자기보다 예쁘거나
키가 커
살아가기 힘든 환경이 되면

주변의 경쟁자를
모조리 제거하기 위해
스스로 부름켜에서 휘발성 오일을 분비하여
함께 분신자살한다

발화점이 35도로
온 산야를 순식간에 불태워버리는 방화광

시스투스는
불에 잘 견디는 씨앗으로
잿더미에서 다시 싹을 틔워
대를 이어 간다.

# Cistus Flower

Blooming white purple pink
Beautiful here
Popular cistus flowers

Plants thrive around
Prettier than you
Tall
When the environment is difficult to live in

Competitors around
To completely remove
By secreting volatile oils from
Commit suicide together

Flash point 35 degrees
An arsonist that burns the entire mountain and field in an instant

Cistus is
Seeds that are resistant to fire
To sprout again from the ashes
Carry on from generation to generation.

# 협죽도꽃

꽃이 포근하고
향기가 강하며
오래 피어 있다

풍성한 분홍색꽃
복숭아꽃을 닮았다

줄기가 대나무와 비슷하고
우후죽순처럼 돋아
울타리로 쓰인다

관상용이나 가로수로 쓰이지만
독초로도 알려져 있다

잎에서 추출된 올레안드린이
심장마비를 일으켜 즉사한다

청산가리보다 강한 독성으로
순식간에 살인 도구로 탈바꿈한다.

# Oleander Flower

Flowers are warm
Strong scent
Bloom for a long time

Abundant pink flower
Resembling a peach blossom

The stems are like bamboo
It sprouts like bamboo shoots
Used as a fence

It is used for ornamental purposes or as a street tree
Also known as poison

Oleandrin extracted from leaves
Cause a heart attack and die instantly

More toxic than cyanide
Transforms into a murder weapon in an instant.

# 금잔화

금빛 찻잔에
금잔화 차 한 잔을

항산화 작용으로
노화 방지 효과

항바이러스 작용으로
면역체계를 촉진

구강, 위, 피부
점막을 보호 복구하고

체내 독소를 해독
호르몬 조절과 살균 작용

안구 건조증, 백내장,
떨어지는 시력에 효과

전립선암, 대장암, 심장질환의 위험을
감소시키는 효과

국화과에 알레르기가 있을 땐
부작용도 있네!

# Marigold

In a golden teacup
A cup of marigold tea

With antioxidant action
Anti-aging effect

With antiviral action
Boost the immune system

Mouth, stomach, skin
Protect and restore mucous membranes

Detoxify the body
Hormonal regulation and bactericidal action

Dry eye syndrome, cataracts
Effect on decreased vision

Risk of prostate cancer, colon cancer and heart disease
Reducing effect

If you are allergic to Asteraceae
There are also side effects!

# 에린지움꽃

가뭄에 강하고
긴 장마를 싫어하는 산형과 식물

남몰래
강인한 인상을 주는 꽃

기쁨과 슬픔의 표현이
서툴러

푸른 꽃잎이 흰색으로 바뀌며
고독이 남긴 긴 여운

꽃대 끝에
솔방울 모양의 두상화(頭狀花)

톱니 같은 이파리로
힘차게 호흡하는 모습

꽃 턱잎이 꽃잎처럼 펼쳐져
꽃송이가
더욱더 화려하고 신비롭네!

# Eringium Flower

Drought-resistant
Umbrella plants that do not like long rainy seasons

Secretly
Flowers that make a strong impression

Expression of joy and sorrow
Clumsy

Blue petals turn White
The long afterglow of loneliness

At the end of the flower stalk
Pinecone-shaped head flower

With serrated leaves
Breathing vigorously

Petals spread out like petals
Blossom
It's even more gorgeous and mysterious!

담배꽃 이야기

# 제5부

# 배롱나무꽃

지역마다 여기저기
산천초목을 붉게 / 물들이고 있다

# 토끼풀꽃

오, 나의 사랑

초교 시절
우리의 사랑을 꽃피울 수 있는 곳

우리의 인연
소중히 할 수 있는 곳
토끼풀꽃이 있는 길가

시기와 질투를 멀리하고
깨달음의 삶을
가꾸어 가는 곳
약속의 땅으로

세 잎 클로버로
목걸이를 만들어 걸어주고
네 잎 클로버로
화관을 씌워주리!

# Shamrock Flower

Oh, my love

Elementary school
A place where our love can blossom

Our relationship
A place to cherish
Roadside with shamrock flowers

Stay away from envy and jealousy
A life of enlightenment
Place to grow
To the promised land

With three leaf clover
Make a necklace and hang it
With four leaf clover
Put on a wreath!

# 배롱나무꽃

파란 하늘에
떠다니는 뭉게구름

한여름 무더위 속에
드물게 보이는 배롱나무꽃
어느 사이에
지천(至賤)으로 널려

지역마다 여기저기
산천초목을 붉게
물들이고 있다

온통 초록 세상에
불그스름한 배롱나무꽃이
한층 더 눈에 띈다

백일을 피는 백일홍나무
읽다가 보니 배롱나무가 되고
잘 웃는다고 간지름나무!

# Barberry Flower

In the blue sky
Floating puffy clouds

In the midsummer heat
Rarely seen banyan tree flowers
In between
Scattered all over the place

All over the region
Turning mountain and river plants red
Dyeing

In a green world
Reddish banyan tree flowers
Stand out more

One hundred days blooming rhododendron
As I read it, I became a pear tree
Tickle tree saying that you smile well!

# 천사의나팔꽃

초록색 꽃받침에
노란색과 연분홍빛을 가진
매력적인 꽃

물을 많이 좋아하는
꺾꽂이 식물

동네 어귀
어디에서도 보일 만큼
사랑을 받는 천사의나팔꽃

지나가는 사람에게
깍듯이 인사를 한다

인사를 하지 않는
눈이 부시게
새하얀 나팔꽃과는
악수하지 마세요!

# Angel's Morning Glory

On green calyx
With yellow and pink
Attractive flowers

Likes a lot of water
Cut plant

Estuary
To be seen anywhere
Angel's Morning Glory Beloved

To passersby
Greet you politely

Not saying goodbye
Dazzling
With the pure white morning glory
Don't shake hands!

# 노루귀꽃

어디에 숨었니?

한여름 무더위
엄동설한
꽃샘추위…

잊고 있었는데

한낮의 따뜻한 봄날
양지바른 쪽에
연분홍 꽃으로 나타나
귀엽게 웃고 있네

산모퉁이 길가에
올망졸망

꽃받침 아래 하얀 솜털
은은한 향기

옛 모습 그대로구나!

# Hepatica Flower

Where did you hide?

Midsummer heat
Heavy snow
Blossom cold···

I forgot

A warm spring day in the middle of the day
On the sunny side
Appears in pale pink flowers
You are smiling cutely

On the roadside at the corner of the mountain
All of a sudden

White fluff under the calyx
Breath

It's just like the old days!

# 국수나무꽃

가느다란 가지에서 피는
노란빛 꽃들이 어우러져
향기를 흩날리고

불그레한 줄기를
늘어뜨리며

탑처럼 생긴 꽃차례를
떠받드는 풍성한 이파리들
나비처럼 날아갈 듯

여름이 되니
산천초목은
산새들의 놀이터가 되고
꽃과 벌들의 장터가 된다

가시덩굴 같은 가지는
울타리로 쓰이고
복부비만 치료에도 효능이 있어
국수나무 차로 하루 한 잔씩!

# Laceshrub Flower

Blooming on slender branches
Yellow flowers together
Scatter the scent

Reddish stems
Hanging down

Tower-like inflorescences
Abundant leaves that hold up
As if flying like a butterfly

It's summer
In the natural scenery
Becoming a playground for wild birds
It becomes a marketplace for flowers and bees

Thorn-like branches
Used as a fence
It is also effective in treating abdominal obesity
One cup a day of Laceshrub Tea!

# 바늘꽃

산들바람이
살랑살랑

고독이 내 마음에
숲을 이루면

괜스레
외로워지고 슬퍼진다

길가 풀숲에
연분홍 바늘꽃이 필 무렵

온통 온몸이
붉은빛을 띠는 여인

그녀에게 취하고 싶다
침몰당하고 싶다.

# Needle Flower

Breeze
Salang salang

Loneliness in my heart
If you make a forest

For nothing
Lonely and sad

On the roadside in the grass
When the pink needles bloom

Whole body
Red-haired woman

I want to get her on her
She wants to be sunk.

# 물망초꽃

졸졸 졸
계곡에 띄운
물망초 꽃다발 하나

여름 내(川)를 타고
바쁜 마음으로
임을 찾아가려나

그대 그리워도
모두가 남의 얼굴

찾을 길 없는 그대
연분홍빛 꽃잎으로
흘러만 가네!

# Forget-me-not Flower

Rippling
Floated in the valley
A bouquet of forget-me-nots

Ride the summer river
With a busy mind
I want to find Im

Even if I miss you
Everyone's face

You can't find
With pink petals
It just flows!

# 파리지옥꽃

눈이 부시도록
파란 하늘에
뭉게구름이 흐르고

초록빛이 그윽한
길 숲의 한낮

긴 꽃대 끝에 하얀 꽃송이들
바람에 한들한들
가루받이하고

저 멀리
맛난 꿀샘의 향기를 따라

살짝 닿자마자
두 잎이 순식간에 닫힌다

대롱대롱 아롱진 눈물
서서히
흔적도 없이 사라진다.

# Fly Hell Flower

To dazzle
In the blue sky
Clouds are flowing

Green
Midday in the forest

White flowers at the end of a long flower stalk
Swaying in the wind
To dust

Far away
Following the scent of the delicious honey spring

As soon as I touch you
Two leaves close in an instant

Tears
Slowly
Disappear without a trace.

# 맥문동꽃

입추(立秋)가 지나
선선한 가을 날씨

산야에 핀 겨우살이풀
보랏빛 추억을 더듬고

엄동설한에도
푸름을 잃지 않는 생명력

맥문동 하면
한약재

즐겁게
복용하다가 보면

몸이 가벼워지고
더욱더 건강해지기도.

# Maekmun-dong Flower

Past the first day of autumn
Cool autumn weather

Mistletoe in the mountains
Groping the purple memories

Even in severe snow
Vitality that does not lose greenness

Maekmun-dong
Herbal medicine

Happily
When taking it

Body becomes lighter
Become more healthy.

# 계요등꽃

바닷가 풀숲에서

자줏빛 줄기
힘찬 곡선을 펼치고

귀여운
자루 모양 꽃송이

활짝 핀 흰 꽃잎이
자줏빛을 에워싸고

푸른 잎
하얀 꽃 오밀조밀
활기 넘친 생명력

자신을 지키려
가까이하면
닭 냄새를 풍기는 듯!

# Paederia Flower

In the grass on the beach

Purple stem
Spread the powerful curve

Cute
Flower stalk

Blooming White petals
Surrounded by purple

Greenery
White flower ryegrass
Vibrant vitality

To protect yourself
If you get close
It smells like chicken!

# 담배꽃 이야기

초판인쇄 2021년 10월 10일  초판발행  2021년 10월 15일

지은이   장현경
펴낸이   장현경  펴낸곳   엘리트출판사
등록일   2013년 2월 22일 제2013-10호

서울특별시 광진구 긴고랑로15길 11 (중곡동)
전화  010-5338-7925
E-mail : wedgus@hanmail.net

정가  11,000원

ISBN  979-11-87573-31-9 03810